4011/23

The Adventures of Finn O'Shea

Book 1

ISBN: 9798566652085

Meet Finn O'Shea… He is smart, he is witty … and he is an **inventor**!

'An inspiring story of courage, determination and resilience.'

Astro Fiasco.

'Finn's Space Adventure'

Illustrated by Mark Beech.

Written by Dr Marian Brennan

Copyright

www.marianbrennan.com

ISBN: 978-1-7399835-0-5

Published by Blackditch Press

For Aoife, Oscar and Kieran.

Thank You's

Thank you to my readers for asking, *'what happens to Finn next?'* A special thanks to Thomás, Sophia, Keyaan, Callum, Alice, Áine-Rose and Maia for your enthusiasm and inspiring feedback. Thank you to all my proofreaders, Aoife, Oscar, Karen, Geraldine, Maia, Glenn, Mom and Dad. Thank you to Grainne Quinlan and Imogen Russell Williams for your very insightful reviews and comments.

To my most enthusiastic supporters, Aoife and Oscar for begging for the next chapter and keeping me writing.

To Anthony, thank you for the endless writing and plot discussions and for always being so supportive.

Contents

Chapter 1: The Journey

As the plane levelled off after take-off, in-flight service began and we started discussing what snacks we were going to order from the trolley.

"Aaaagh!" everyone screamed together.

It was high-pitched and loud! Adrenaline

pulsed through my veins, making my heart race. Before the cart could get to us, my laptop went flying and my seatbelt went tight digging into my stomach as I lifted off my seat.

"This is your Captain speaking, we are experiencing some turbulence, please stay…" he broke off and didn't finish his sentence.

The plane suddenly dropped again.

"Aaaagh!" everyone screamed together again. Then they all said, *"ssshhh!"* like everyone wanted the captain to be able to concentrate. The plane seemed a little out of control bumping and bucking all over the place! I looked around and realized I was gripping Kristina's arm so tightly that my

knuckles had turned white, and everyone around me was really pale… even the adults! The whole plane was silent with everyone wide-eyed.

Not everyone had buckled up before the turbulence and I could see a man who had a cut on his forehead. He was trying to get back to his seat, but the plane was still like a bucking bronco. The trolley was loose and speeding down the aisle, bashing into seats.

"Keep your arms in!" I shouted as the cart careered towards us. Just in time Jean-Luca and my mom pulled their arms in.

The plane climbed again and we were thrust back into our seats. I thought I might be sick!

As quick as the chaos had started, it ended as we glided out of the turbulence.

"You see," I groaned to Jean-Luca and Kristina... "flying is *NOT* safe!"

"If you don't like this, you are not going to enjoy the flight simulator at the space centre," said Jean-Luca with a grin.

"That is *totally* different," I said.

"I can't believe we are going to watch your rocket launching into space!" said Kieran.

My friends had helped me with my rocket, so we had all been invited to watch the launch together. We had worked on the model rocket for over a year before it finally worked, going on to win the Young Scientist Competition.

Kristina and Kieran seemed to be enjoying themselves on the flight, but I did not like flying. We had been invited to the launch of the rocket I had designed, so we didn't have much choice. We couldn't exactly take a bus from Ireland to the USA.

"Why didn't Aoife come with us?" asked Kieran who liked playing with my little sister.

"My mom thought it wouldn't be fun for Aoife," I said.

"Why?" asked Kristina.

"It is very hard for her to sit still for so long on the plane, and hotels are not much fun for toddlers," I said.

"So, who's looking after her?" asked Kristina.

"She's staying with my cousins while we are in Orlando, so I'm sure she's going to have lots of fun!"

Our conversation was cut short when Jean-Luca's dad got up to help the man who had cut his head.

Jean-Luca's parents had come along as Jean-Luca's mom was a lawyer. She had helped us to patent my rocket design. She would be meeting with the team at the space centre and looking after all the 'legal stuff' to make sure my design was *'legally'* protected.

The in-flight attendants were trying to help right the cart and were quickly getting the first-aid kit. Even though everyone looked quite flustered, it was like a well-rehearsed play with everyone knowing exactly what to do without saying a word.

"This is your captain speaking, the turbulence experienced was due to unexpected pockets of low pressure."

"We have increased our altitude and we do not expect further turbulence."

"We will be landing in Orlando in 1 hour and forty-five minutes."

The seatbelt light went off.

No one unclicked their seatbelts!

"I think I'll keep my seatbelt on," I said.

"What if you need to pee?" asked Jean-Luca.

"Coke bottle?" I said with a grin, and we all started laughing.

Chapter 2: Hotel motel

The hotel was not like any hotel I had ever seen. In fact, we hardly ever went to hotels as my parents preferred camping and renting houses when we went away on holiday. It was more like the motels that you saw on

TV shows. My dad parked our car outside our room.

"This place is *SO* cool!" I said, jumping out of the car.

My parents had booked a 'suite' with 3 rooms that were joined together. We collected the keys and we all ran upstairs to check out the rooms. The beds were so big!

"I've never seen such a **giant** bed!" exclaimed Jean-Luca.

Kristina threw herself onto the bed lying sideways and stretching out her arms.

"I don't even touch the sides," she said and we all started laughing.

The adults arrived... "Please can we share the middle room?" I asked.

"Please, please, please?" we begged together.

"Sure," said mom, with a smirk.

"Yay!" We all started jumping around.

"It's going to be like a giant sleepover," said Kristina.

"As long as you all promise to go to sleep at 8 o'clock?"

"Sure," "Yes," "Of course," we all said with our fingers crossed behind our backs, giggling.

The adults started organising luggage, dropping it into different rooms.

"Come on, let's go get something to eat," said mom.

I was suddenly *very* hungry.

We walked down past the pool.

"This is such a cool hotel!" said Kieran.

"Can we swim after dinner?" asked Jean-Luca.

"There's a jacuzzi!" shouted Kristina running over to take a look.

It was surrounded on one side by trees and shrubs, making it feel like it was in a jungle.

We sat by the pool and ordered milkshakes and burgers. The milkshakes were bigger than anything I had ever seen. I had a lime flavoured milkshake.

"A green milkshake?" said Jean-Luca in disgust.

"It's out of this world!" I said, sipping the milkshake and rolling my eyes into the back of my head with a heavenly feeling like I might go into a trance.

Kristina had ordered a halloumi burger, as she was vegetarian.

"This is *soooo good!*" she said taking an enormous bite.

The burgers were so big that none of us could finish them... not even the adults!

The waiter came out to ask if there was a problem with the food.

"Not at all," said my dad. "The food was delicious! Just a little too much."

"Would you like it to go?" he asked.

The thought of cold burgers and chips later was not very appealing.

"No thank you," said my father reading the faces around the table.

I leaned back in my chair, my stomach sticking out.

"Perhaps we can share portions next time or ask for half portions so that we don't waste food," said my dad.

"That is an excellent idea," said my mom.

"Please can we swim now?" asked Jean-Luca.

"After that meal! You'll drown!" said his mom.

"What about the jacuzzi?" persisted Jean-Luca.

"I suppose that would be OK," said his mom.

We ran up to our room to change, ripping open our suitcases to find our swimsuits. The adults stayed out on the deck having drinks while we played in the jacuzzi.

There were three different bubble functions and it was so lovely and warm.

"This is amazing!" said Kieran.

"Look up!" shouted Kristina.

A rocket was being launched and we had a perfect view from the jacuzzi.

"It does not get better than this!" said Jean-Luca.

"Look the booster is kicking in," said Kristina.

The first thruster started to fall away and the second thruster kicked in, with huge jets of fire!

"I can't believe we are going to the space centre tomorrow!" I said, gazing into the sky.

"It's like a dream come true!"

Chapter 3: Trainee astronauts

"Up, up, up, everyone..."

"Today's the day!" said my dad.

Jean-Luca was rubbing his eyes and Kristina was fumbling around, looking for her glasses.

I jumped out of bed and stretched.

"Chop, chop!" said my dad. "Get dressed, so we don't miss out on breakfast!"

The sound of clinking cutlery could be heard before we got to the breakfast room. The smells were delicious! Bacon, coffee and something sweet!

Our waiter came over and asked, "what can I get for you?"

I had no idea what to say and quickly started scanning the menu. The adults started ordering coffee. I elbowed Kieran and grinned.

"We can have pancakes for breakfast!"

After only 5 minutes, a huge stack of pancakes arrived with bacon and maple syrup.

"I love America already!" said Jean-Luca, through forkfuls of pancake.

Again, we could not finish our food and 'rolled' out of the restaurant. After a quick stop to brush our teeth and grab our things, we were in the car on the way to the space centre.

Mom and dad were scanning their phones for details about where to go and what to do. We were stuck in traffic, so I just stared out the window trying to remember everything. It was all so different to Ireland. The roads were much wider and the buildings much bigger and everything seemed to be much faster!

Arriving at the space centre we needed to show our identification and invitation at the gate. There was a guard dressed in full military uniform who did not want to allow us through.

"Children are not allowed on-site at this facility, Mam," he said, with a severe look on his face.

My mom was searching the cubby hole frantically for the invitation letter.

"But we have a meeting," she said. "My son helped design the new rocket being tested today," she explained.

The guard looked into the back of the car.

"Sure, he did!"

"I'm afraid I'm going to have to ask you to back up, Mam,"

"We're going to be late!" I said to Jean-Luca, Kristina and Kieran.

"We're going to miss everything!"

My mom found the letter.

"Can you call General James O'Brien?" she said handing over the piece of paper.

He pressed the button on his radio.

"Yes, sir…."

"of course, sir…"

"I'll let them through right away."

"Sometimes kids, it's not what you know, it's **who** you know!" grinned my mom as we cruised through the gate.

We sped up to the main building, where the General was waiting to meet us. There was a woman standing next to him wearing jeans, a T-shirt and a red cap.

"Welcome!" said the General, "It is so fantastic to have you here for the launch today."

The adults shook hands and thanked the General for meeting us.

"This is Jade, our lead programme specialist," said the General. "She is going to show you around."

"I want her job," said Jean-Luca to me under his breath.

"I'm going to take you on a tour of our production facility," said Jade.

"Finn, I want you to understand every aspect of our production process."

The tour started in the factory where rocket components were in various stages of building and testing. It was incredible, but also really noisy!

I was really interested in everything, so it took us ages to get through the factory.

"Did you see all those amazing machines?" I asked Kristina and Jean-Luca.

"I wish we had more time!" I said

"Did you see the enormous metal panels being made for the new rockets?" asked Kieran who had wandered off in a different direction.

"No," we all said together.

"They are HUGE!!!" said Kieran.

"Imagine how cool it would be to work here!?!" said Kristina.

"Why do you need to have so many spare parts?" Kieran asked Jade.

"We have been having trouble with the landing of the boosters," said Jade, "..so we have to keep making new ones for each launch."

"We want to reuse them, but they fall over or land at an angle, 9 times out of 10, exploding in a ball of fire!"

"It is getting *really, really* expensive!"

"That sounds like it could be a coding problem," I suggested.

"You kids can also code?" asked Jade astounded.

"Well of course," said Kristina, "all of the inventions that we made needed controllers and so we had to learn to code to make them work."

"We have all been coding for years!" I said, remembering all the coding summer camps I'd been sent to.

"If you want we can take a look at your code and see if we can help," said Jean-Luca.

"It would be great if you could take a look at it, but first we need to get over to the training centre," said Jade. "You kids are joining the astronaut training today."

Jean-Luca, Kristina and Kieran were beaming smiles... I on the other hand was feeling a bit queasy at the thought... I had heard people sometimes passed out in the simulators.

"Don't worry," said Jade seeing my face... "They'll go easy on you lot because you're kids."

Kristina looked a bit disappointed... she was a bit of a daredevil and loved all things exciting and borderline dangerous. She loved rollercoasters, mountain biking, rock climbing and just about anything that involved speed.

As we arrived at the training centre, we could see the astronauts in the zero-gravity simulator floating around trying to do tasks like writing on a notepad to communicate. One of the astronauts had lost his notepad and pencil and was trying to swim through the air after it.

Jade let us try out the zero-gravity simulator straight away. We stepped into the chamber and immediately felt weightless. It was a weird feeling. We were bumping into the sides and into each other. Each bump sent us off in opposite directions.

"This is AWESOME!" shouted Kieran.

There was a station set up with objects and tasks, such as writing a note and fixing an electrical panel with a screwdriver. It took about 10 minutes just to get to the task station, and it was nearly impossible to do even these simple tasks.

After floating around in the simulator for about 20 minutes, Jade gestured to us to go over to her. We were ushered towards a changing room, where we were each given an astronaut suit.

"These have been made especially for you all," said Jade.

The suits had each of our names on them.

"What? This is incredible!" I said, running my finger over my name badge that was stitched into my suit.

"Come on, suit up, we're on a bit of a tight schedule here," said Jade, smiling at them.

We started quickly putting the suits on. There was an underlayer that was easy enough to put on and quite comfortable. The outer layer was bulkier, and it was quite hard to bend over to get the boots on. It reminded me of when we went to the ice-skating rink and put on the awkward *'for hire'* skates that are inflexible and hard to adjust.

"OK, time to get those helmets on and to do a comms check," said Jade.

We put our helmets on. It felt like we were putting fishbowls on our heads, but they were padded on the inside with a hidden mic for communication. It was all surprisingly quite light.

"Soundcheck time," said Jade, "Kristina can you hear me?"

"This is totally rad!" said Kristina.

"I'll take that as a yes, but next time let's try 'Roger that, Jade'."

Jean-Luca started laughing. "Am I talking to Roger or Jade?"

"Roger that Jean-Luca," said Jade.

None of us could stop laughing now.

"Finn, can you hear me?"

"Roger that, Jade," I spluttered, trying very hard not to laugh.

"OK you bunch of jokers, over to the flight simulator," said Jade with a grin.

Chapter 4: Flying high!

When we were done with the chamber, we were ushered straight over to the flight simulator and given a lesson on how to control the rocket in the simulator. It was like video games in arcades where you climb into a chair to play. It felt really real though, with lots of buttons and levers. The instructors gave brief instructions on the controls and then we all watched a video tutorial sitting in our own rocket simulator. We all had microphones in our helmets to communicate with each other and the control centre.

"This is amazing!" shouted Kristina.

The countdown started:

"10, 9.."

"8, 7..." I jiggled in my seat getting comfortable.

"6, 5..." Kristina was ready.

"4, 3..." Jean-Luca closed his eyes.

"2,1..." We all braced ourselves.

We were thrust backwards hard into our seats and the seats started to shake. There was a really loud rumbling noise.

"This feels so real!" I said over the comms, once the noise died down a little.

"It is an exact replica of the cockpit of the rocket we are launching this evening," said Jade over the comms.

"There are sooooo many buttons!" shouted Kieran.

"You don't need to shout Kieran... you're hurting my ears!" I said.

Our rockets stabilized, levelled off and we were flying through the dark night sky.

"This is so beautiful and peaceful, I just want to stay here forever," I said breathing a sigh of relief that I had not been sick during the flight simulator 'take-off'.

"Let's do the meteor field training session," said Jean-Luca.

"OK, but after that, I want to try the engine loss and landing one," said Kieran.

"There is enough time to do two training sessions," said Jade through the comms.

"Those two are good choices," said Jade.

We dodged most of the meteors, but when we hit one, it felt like a real bump shaking the entire chair violently. Then the control system started to flash and beep a warning.

"This is like the best video game ever!" shouted Jean-Luca.

"You really don't need to shout, Jean Luca!" said Kristina.

An electronic notification came over our comms.

"20-minute simulation time remaining,"

"I don't want this to end, this is so much fun!" I moaned.

"Me neither," said Kristina.

"Damage to Thruster 1," came the automatic voice.

"Shutting down thruster 1," said the voice.

I pressed a button that said 'engage emergency thruster'.

My simulator started to rumble and shake and then I was flung backwards into my seat. The force was so strong from this burst of speed and I did not have enough time to avoid all the meteorites.

I thought I might be sick in my helmet again, but there was no time to think about that, as the rocket was shaking violently and I was trying to get it under control.

"I've hit a meteorite!" I shouted into my comms.

'Fatal damage' flashed up in red on the control panel.

"We have detected a reduction in pressure in the cabin. Would you like to initiate the emergency landing protocol?" came the calm automatic voice over the comms.

I looked around for the button.

I found one that said: "Emergency landing"

Without hesitation, I hit the button.

I battled to get the rocket under control, the comms team gave me instructions about how to stabilize my rocket.

"Reduce your power on thruster 2," said the voice.

I was shouting over the loud sound of the rocket engine while I was spinning around and shaking.

"I'm going to be sick," I said.

"Breathe deeply Finn," said Jade in a calm voice.

"You got this."

I zoned out and listened to the controller, focussing only on the voice and following the instructions exactly. The spinning and shaking finally slowed and stopped.

"Good, now level off…"

"You need to point the nose of the rocket upwards, and reduce the thruster power a bit more."

"Steady, now," said Jade.

In the last seconds, my stomach lurched like I was going over a big bump in a car, the speed reduced and then suddenly there was loud noise again, bumping and rocking and I had landed. I sat frozen for a few seconds and then started unclipping my seatbelt. This was hard to do with the big gloves, but I finally managed to release it. The door to the simulator opened and Jade helped me out. I could barely stand!

"Take it easy for a few minutes," said Jade as she helped me out of my helmet.

"I don't feel too good," I groaned.

"That was excellent!" she said. "You did really well to get your rocket under control!"

Jean-Luca and Kieran staggered over laughing.

"We both crash-landed our rockets," they said in hysterics.

Kristina walked up with her helmet under her arm looking the picture of composure, like a real astronaut.

"That was so *incredible!*" she said with a little skip, grinning from ear to ear.

"How many asteroids did you hit?" asked Kieran.

"None," said Kristina with a straight face.

"What?" said the boys together.

"None," said Kristina, "I had a perfect flight!"

"OK," said Jade. "Well done!"

"Nobody chundered, and you're all still standing."

"Only just!" I said under my breath, still feeling a bit wobbly.

"We have to get moving," said Jade.

"Stay in your suits and we can get some pics next to the rocket with the astronauts leaving today," she said.

Kieran and Jean-Luca high fived and started walking ahead replaying the simulator experience. I was still trying to steady myself.

"You OK?" asked Kristina.

"Not really... I feel a bit wobbly."

She linked her arm through mine.

"We can walk slowly in the fresh air," she said.

"Looking far away at the horizon always helps when I get motion sickness," said Kristina.

"You get motion sickness?" I asked surprised.

"It can happen to anyone," she said.

"Even experienced sailors can get seasick sometimes."

"Come on! We need to be quick now as the launch is happening in less soon," said Jade.

Chapter 5: Spaceman

It was a long walk over to the launch pad where the rocket was being prepared for launch. There were a lot of people doing last-minute checks. Helmets under our arms, Jade walked us straight over to the rocket. We were following in real astronauts' footsteps! We walked down a long corridor and got into the elevator to go up to the cockpit. There was a wall with astronauts' signatures from all those that had gone into space before. This rocket had a crew of four and they were going up to the space station to deliver supplies, materials for repairs, and new equipment for the biological research laboratory.

This was the first launch of the rocket with my design that was going into space with astronauts on board. This made me really curious about how well they had implemented my design. I had not been able to see any of the test rockets, except via online video call, which really was not the same.

After we had met the astronauts and got their autographs, Jade said we could go ahead and have a look around the rocket.

"There is only half an hour before the launch now, so you only have 10 minutes in the rocket."

I must have looked disappointed.

"Sorry Finn, we will need you all out in 10 minutes so that we can do the last checks with the astronauts," said Jade.

"OK," I said.

"We'll be out in a few minutes."

"I have a few things to do now before the launch," said Jade.

"Meet you all back at the viewing point in 10 minutes."

"Sure," said Kristina.

"Thanks, Jade," I said.

"Where's the viewing point?" asked Kieran

"Just over there," said Jean-Luca.

"Where all those people are gathering," said Kristina.

"Where did they all come from?" asked Kieran.

"They are family of the astronauts and some of the staff from the base control centre," said Jean-Luca. "Didn't you listen to anything in the briefing earlier?"

"I was way too excited!" Kieran said, looking around.

"This is **incredible!**" said Kristina again.

Kieran, Jean-Luca and Kristina had a quick look around and then sat in the cockpit pretending to be astronauts launching into space.

I went into the back of the rocket to check everything out. I wanted to know everything about how the rocket worked. It was incredible to see how everything was packed away neatly and all the supplies were so organised. There was everything needed to survive. There was also a door or small hatch to the one side of the rear section of the rocket. The hatch had a lever with no warnings, so I opened it and went in. It was a second reserve rocket attached to the main rocket with a full cockpit and even more supplies. I sat down in the cockpit, enjoying the quiet, relaxing and trying to soak it all in. It had all happened so fast, and now here I was sitting in a real rocket that I had designed! It really was a dream come true. I closed my eyes, imagining what it would feel like to be launching into space.

In the main cockpit, Jean-Luca, Kieran and Kristina were meeting the astronauts again. They all looked so happy and relaxed, although they must have been a little nervous about blasting into space.

"It was lovely meeting you all, but you are going to have to go to the viewing area now as we do our final checks," said Andy, one of the astronauts.

The captain's name was Lerato. She had a really big smile and said, "when you are older, you can also be astronauts, if you work hard."

"Remember," she said, "the sky is really *not* the limit!"

And with a wink, she put her helmet on.

Jean-Luca, Kristina and Kieran left the main cockpit and waved goodbye as they got into the lift.

Over the main loudspeakers and helmet comms an announcement boomed:

"Final check protocol commencing."

"All visitors and staff please move to the viewing areas."

I heard the announcement and moved towards the exit of the reserve rocket.

In the main cockpit, the astronauts were doing the final checks.

"Closing all cabin doors," said Captain Lerato.

"Visual check complete," said Andy.

The door between the escape rocket and the main rocket sealed shut with a click. I tried to open it, but it was electronically sealed for the launch. My heart started to race. I banged on the door hoping the astronauts would hear me, but the engines had been started and the noise was too loud.

"OK, Finn... Think!"

"Use the comms!"

I was now talking to myself out loud. I put on my helmet and tried the comms.

At the viewing point, about a hundred people were trying to watch the launch. Everyone was pushed up against the barrier trying to get the best view.

"Jean-Luca, where's Finn?" asked Finn's dad.

"I don't know," said Jean-Luca shouting over the noise.

"He didn't come down with us," said Kristina.

"I'm sure he is here somewhere," said Kieran.

They all looked around for a bit, but there was a lot of noise and excitement. The countdown started over the loudspeaker:

"10, 9, 8...

...7, 6, 5, 4...

3, 2, 1..."

The roar of the engines sounded like a massive explosion. The cloud of smoke from the thrusters was so big that at first, they could hardly see the rocket at all until it got off the ground.

In the rocket, I barely got myself strapped in in time for the launch. The G-force from the launch was incredible. I thought I might become part of the seat and never be able to be separated again!

It all happened so fast that I had not really realised that I was going into space!

As we left the Earth's atmosphere, I was momentarily overwhelmed with the view. To be looking back down on Earth and seeing the vastness of space was incredible. I was in awe! It was so unbelievably big and I felt so unbelievably small!

I was now too scared to press any buttons in case I jettisoned myself off into space separating from the main rocket. I realised that nobody knew I was still in the reserve rocket!

All of a sudden, my comms came to life!

"Finn, can you hear us?"

"I can hear you loud and clear," I said.

"Finn, can you hear us? Over..."

"Yes, I can hear you," I said a bit louder.

"Finn, can you hear us?" came the question again.

I realised that they could not hear me. I looked around and saw there was another comms button in the middle of the console.

"What else could 'comms' mean?" I thought.

I pressed the button and my comms started working.

"I'm so sorry," I said, my voice cracking.

"Finn, is that you?" asked Captain Lerato confused.

"Yes, it's me," I said.

"Where *exactly* are you?" asked Captain Lerato.

The engines were still blasting at full throttle so it was hard to hear her.

"I think I am in the reserve rocket," I said.

"DO NOT TOUCH ANYTHING!" she said severely.

I held up my hands, moving them as far away from the buttons as possible!

"Not touching anything!" I said.

After the engines quietened down and we were cruising, Andy came in through the hatch.

"What on Earth did you think you were doing!?!?" said Andy.

Well, we were not really on Earth anymore I thought, but I could see that this was not really the time to point this out from the look on Andy's face.

"I didn't do it on purpose.." I said.

"Sure," said Andy, not looking impressed.

"I… I.." I started to stutter.

Andy cut me off.

"Come on let's go and talk to the captain," he said shaking his head.

I followed Andy to the main cockpit feeling like I was in really big trouble now! It really was a bit of a situation, as there was no going back now!

I could hear Captain Lerato talking to the control room at the base station down on Earth.

"Yes, we've found him,"

"He was in the reserve escape rocket,"

"No. I don't know how he got there,"

"He's here now," said Captain Lerato.

I was now pretty terrified that I was going to be in a super amount of trouble.

"Finn said he *'accidentally'* got trapped in the escape rocket," said Andy with irritation in his voice.

Captain Lerato must have seen the fear on my face.

"So…" she said, thinking for a moment. "Do you have an explanation?"

I started to babble really fast about exactly what had happened, barely stopping to breathe.

Captain Lerato put her hand up breaking into a smile, a little amused at the situation.

"Well, Finn O'Shea, you are officially the world's youngest astronaut!"

"Welcome to space!" she said with a grin.

Chapter 6: The giraffe snatcher

As soon as the adults realised Finn was in the rocket, Jean-Luca, Kieran and Kristina were sent straight back to the hotel with Jean-Luca's dad. It was all over the news "10-

year-old rocket designer stows away at rocket launch!"

"But that's not true!" shouted Kristina at the TV.

"The news always lies!" said Kieran slumping back on the bed.

"Now what are we going to do?" asked Jean-Luca. "The whole holiday is ruined!"

"Have you thought about Finn at all?" asked Kristina.

"He must be terrified!"

"Or having the time of his life!" said Jean-Luca.

"This is a dream come true for him!"

"He's having a blast up there and we're trapped in this hotel room until he gets back!" said Jean-Luca throwing himself onto the bed.

"Why don't we play cards," suggested Kieran, "I have a new game 'Rocket, Asteroid, Splat'," he said bursting into laughter.

"Aaagh! OK," said Jean-Luca, resigning himself to a long wait.

We kept the TV on, with the news rolling, hoping for updates about Finn. After what felt like our hundredth game of Kieran's card game, 'Rocket, Asteroid, Splat!', a news story came on about a missing baby giraffe. The story explained that the baby giraffe had been stolen!

"How is it even possible to steal a giraffe?" asked Kieran.

" .. and why?" asked Kristina incredulously!

The story went on to say that the baby giraffe had not yet been weaned, and therefore it needed its mother and that if it was not returned soon, it may die.

"How can there be such evil people in the world?" asked Kristina.

The children were really bored being cooped up in the hotel room! The news had been on continuously and Jean-Luca's dad had been super stressed waiting for updates. They weren't allowed to go anywhere as they needed to be *'supervised'*, and Jean-Luca's dad was busy changing flights and hotel bookings and was constantly on the phone to Finn's parents and Jean-Luca's mom, who were still at the base station.

"Come on dad?" said Jean-Luca. "Can't we at least go to the pool?"

"No. You need to be supervised at the pool, and I need to sort all of the flights out, and contact work and we don't know when we will be going home. All of our bookings need to change."

"*Aaagh!*" moaned Jean-Luca.

"You just need to sit tight a little bit longer," he said.

The story about the giraffe was still on the news and it turned out the people who stole her wanted a ransom for her return. Immediately, the company gave a statement that they wanted proof that the giraffe was alive. The criminals responded by posting pictures of the giraffe in different locations every few hours.

"This is so wrong!" said Kristina.

Kristina was really into animals and nature and this case had really upset her.

"How can someone do this?" exclaimed Kristina.

"That baby giraffe is going to die if they can't find her."

"If you feel that way, why don't we do something?" said Kieran.

"What can we do?" asked Jean-Luca. "We are locked into a hotel room and the jailor is my dad!"

"We are all coders and these guys are leaving clues all over the internet!" said Kieran.

"You are right!" said Kristina. "Of course!"

Kristina started digging in her suitcase looking for her tablet. Kieran had pulled out his laptop and Jean-Luca was already knocking on his dad's door to get a device as well.

"OK, so what do we have?" asked Kieran.

"Well, he is mobile which means either a truck or a train," said Kristina.

"Most likely a small truck, as he had to get the baby giraffe out of the park, and there are no train lines into the park," said Jean-Luca.

"If we can find out which road he is on, the police can set up a roadblock," said Kristina all fired up.

"Download all the pictures he has uploaded," said Kieran.

"Why?" asked Jean-Luca.

"Because sometimes people leave their geolocation in the metadata of the file by accident when they upload the photo," explained Kieran.

"Surely the giraffe snatcher wouldn't be that stupid!" said Kristina.

"You would be surprised how many people forget to 'clean' their pictures before uploading them," said Kieran.

"How do you know so much about this?" asked Jean-Luca.

"Well, my mom is obsessed about making sure our location is not on any photos that we share and my dad wants to keep the location on so that he can have a timeline of where we've been... you can see where I'm going with this!"

"Let's just say it is discussed a lot in our house!" said Kieran.

"Nothing!" said Kristina after a few minutes.

"They're all clean!"

"OK...." said Kieran.

"Well then let's blow up each of these pics on the screen and see what clues we can get from the background."

"The background is a bit blurry in this first one. Anyone got software to enhance the pictures?" asked Kristina.

"I do," said Kieran.

They started going through the zoomed-in pictures one at a time. After what seemed like hours of going through every pixel of the first two pictures, they had nothing.

"Dinner time!" called Jean-Luca's dad.

They went down to the pool area and ordered the same food as before, big milkshakes and burgers and chips. It had been a really intense day! Jean-Luca's mom joined them mid-way through the meal.

They all started asking questions at the same time.

"When is Finn coming back?" asked Kristina.

"Is Finn in trouble?" asked Jean-Luca.

"What are they going to do to him?" asked Kieran.

Jean-Luca's mom put her hand up. "It's been a long day," she said with a yawn.

"Finn is safe and he is not in any trouble for now, but we don't know much."

"Can we talk to him?" asked Kristina.

"Not at the moment sweetheart, maybe in the next few days."

Jean-Luca's mom did not seem to be open to any more questions. Everyone ate in silence. It should not have been like this. It had been the best day of their lives, and now perhaps also the worst.

"Can we have a short jacuzzi," asked Jean-Luca.

"Of course," said his mother distracted.

Since they managed to get no information about Finn, they carried on chatting about the case of the missing baby giraffe.

"What do you call a baby giraffe anyway?" asked Kieran to No one in particular.

"A calf," said Kristina.

"Are you sure?" asked Kieran.

The look on her face said it all.

"OK... OK!" said Kieran with his hands up.

"So, where are we?" asked Kieran.

"Nowhere really... we've got nothing," said Kristina.

"Don't be like that, we have just eliminated one path," said Kieran. "There are still lots of clues."

Another kid arrived at the jacuzzi. "Can I swim with y'all?" she asked with a strong American accent.

"Sure," said Kieran and Jean-Luca together.

"My name is Alyssa," she said jumping in.

"Kieran, Kristina and Jean-Luca," said Kieran introducing them all.

"You guys aren't from here, are you?" she said.

"How did you know?" asked Kristina.

"Your names and your accents."

"We're from Ireland," said Kieran.

"Oh!" she said. "That kid that went into space is from Ireland..." she said trailing off.

"Yeh! We're with him!" said Kristina.

"For real?" she asked.

"Yeh, for real," said Kieran.

"I have a thousand questions," said Alyssa.

"So do we," said Kieran.

"But No one is telling us anything!" said Jean-Luca exasperated.

"Hotels are so boring!" she said after a pause, not knowing what else to say.

"Do you spend a lot of time in hotels?" asked Kristina.

"Not normally," said Alyssa, "but my dad just got a new job here and our house is not ready yet, so we are going to be here for at least another 2 weeks."

"How long have you been here?"

"Only one week." she said, "but there haven't been any kids around."

"Well, you can hang with us because I think we might be here a while," said Kristina.

Alyssa put the bubbles on and started giggling as Jean-Luca nearly jumped out of his skin.

"So, if you know about Finn… you have been watching the news," said Kristina.

"Yes… there's pretty much nothing else to do around here," she said.

"Well, what do you think about the missing baby giraffe?" asked Jean-Luca.

"It is awful! The calf is going to starve if they don't find him soon," exclaimed Alyssa.

"We have been doing some investigating, but we don't know Orlando very well," said Kristina.

"We're tracking the giraffe thief," said Jean-Luca. "Analysing all the pictures to find out where he is, and where he's going."

"That calf is only going to survive for about a week if we don't find it," said Kristina.

"The thief has to be mobile and there are only three major routes out of the park. Going at a max of 80 miles an hour with a giraffe in tow, he could not be all that far," said Alyssa. "So, Route 4 north or south or..." she continued.

"You're in!" Kristina burst out.

"What do you mean?" asked Alyssa.

"We're investigating the case of the missing giraffe," said Kristina.

"Meet us at breakfast tomorrow and we can start working on the maps," said Kieran.

As exciting as the project was, they were all so exhausted from the day at the space centre that they could barely keep their eyes open. They headed back to their room, brushed their teeth, put on pyjamas and climbed into bed. Usually, there would be lots of chatter and banter, but not tonight! Within seconds, the sound of deep breathing was all that could be heard in the room.

Chapter 7: The space station

After a short while flying, I could see something that looked like a cluster of stars at first. I had been allowed to stay upfront in the main cockpit. I was not sure if they were being nice to me, or if they were just worried

I might push buttons in the escape pod and jettison myself off into space by accident.

"What's that?" I asked.

"That's where we're headed Finn, the international space station," said Captain Lerato.

"It's huge!" I said.

"It's pretty incredible, alright," said Captain Lerato. "You'd better buckle up, we'll be docking soon."

I turned to go back to the reserve rocket.

"No," said Captain Lerato. "You stay here."

"Andy, could you go to the reserve rocket?" she asked.

"I think I'll keep an eye on this guy from now on!" she said with a wink.

I didn't mind at all, as this meant I got the best view of docking into the space station.

"This is Captain Lerato of the US F. O'Shea, requesting permission to dock, over."

"Roger that."

"Great to have you joining us, permission granted."

"Please proceed to docking station B."

"Proceeding to docking station B," said Captain Lerato.

"I need to let you know that we have a minor ride along!"

"I don't think I got that… Did you say you have a **child** on board!?!?"

"That is correct."

"We have 10-year-old Finn O'Shea with us, who designed the rocket we are flying in!"

"Copy that!"

I smiled meekly feeling a little awkward and not knowing quite what to expect.

The rocket rounded the station where docking station B was clearly signposted. Captain Lerato slowed the engines and used reverse thrusters to gently manoeuvre the rocket into its 'parking' space. With a small jolt, the rocket's motion stopped. The door hatches were now connected to the space station and sealed tightly to the side of it. We unclipped, and Captain Lerato said, "Docking protocol complete."

"Permission for the crew to come aboard."

"Permission granted, over."

"Roger that, over."

"You ready for this Finn?"

"Not what I had planned for this evening...
but this has been one of my dreams my whole
life!"

"Let's go," she said with a smile.

The hatch opened and we all floated into
the space station. I had not had much
training, so I kept on bumping into things! We
met the crew one at a time. There was not a
lot of space, so we all floated through one at a
time. There were twelve crew members from
around the world on board.

"You have arrived at just the right time, it's
nearly dinner time," said Jo who was one of
the American crew.

"Are you hungry?" asked Captain Lerato.

I had not had any training in how to manage
water and food in zero gravity. Dinner was

going to be a challenge, but I had a bigger problem right now. I *really* needed to go to the *toilet!*

"Uh, Captain Lerato," I said hesitantly, "How do you go to the toilet in zero gravity?"

"Oh my!" she said. "I forgot that you haven't completed astronaut training!"

"Andy, could you show Finn how the toilet works?"

Andy rolled his eyes.

"Come on then," he said.

I was mortified and wished the space station could swallow me up.

It turned out that this was a real danger as the toilet had a suction function! There was a

tube for number one's and a separate tube for
number two's, and it was really complicated!

You needed to keep the suction on to catch
every last drop of pee before taking it off. I
got most of my pee down the pee tube but

missed a few drops, that then floated off up into the air!

"Uh oh!" I said trying to catch the pee drops with some tissues before they hit the wall and roof. It was like trying to catch bubbles, but while floating around yourself. As I struggled to catch the pee drops, I kept colliding into the walls.

"You OK in there?" asked Andy, who could hear me bumping into the walls.

"All good," I called back catching the last bubble drop of pee.

I was relieved coming out of the toilet, but at the same time terrified for when I might need to do a number 2!

"OK, let's go get something to eat," said Andy.

Captain Lerato handed me two silver packets, one of which had a straw. I held onto them, but did nothing yet, just waited to see what the others did. The bag with the straw seemed to be water, and others were drinking directly from the tube. Captain Lerato squeezed out a droplet of water and caught it in her mouth. I had already had enough of droplets floating off, so I just used the straw.

"Do you like jambalaya?" asked Jo.

I looked blank. I had no idea what Jo was asking me.

"Mm hmm," I said, not sure what else to say.

I had never had jambalaya, but I immediately loved it! As I ate, I was trying to identify all the flavours. It was a mixture of sausages and rice and tomato sauce with a few other vegetables. I was not normally a fan of vegetables, but this was amazing. It was sticky enough to eat with a spoon, but still a bit challenging if any bits started to float away.

"This is incredible!" I said.

"As far as space food goes, jambalaya is pretty good," agreed Jo.

"If you think this is good, you should try a real Orlando Jambalaya when you are back on Earth."

"Jambalaya is not 'a thing' in Ireland," I said.

"What do you mean, 'not a thing'?" asked Dave who had joined the conversation.

"Well, it's not on the menu," I said, eating another spoonful. "This is really good!"

"So why don't you tell us how you ended up here on our space station?" said Jo with a grin.

"Well, it's a really long story!" I said.

"We've got time," said Jo.

"OK," I said.

"When I was 8-years old, I was obsessed with rockets and space and I made myself a remote-controlled rocket."

"I won the Young Scientist Competition and the space agency decided to use my design for the new rocket that we came in today."

"So that is why it is called the US F. O'Shea," added Captain Lerato.

"But that does not explain how you got here," said Jo. "They would never have authorised a child to be sent into space!"

"Well, because the rocket was my design, we were allowed to look around the rocket before the launch,"

"... and.." probed Jo.

"... and the door to the reserve rocket sealed and locked me in just before the launch and I couldn't get out!"

"Well, you're here now, so come on and help us unload the supplies from the rocket," said Captain Lerato.

We started unloading the rocket and I helped to take some laboratory supplies to the research lab.

"Hi, I'm Charlie," said the scientist looking after the lab.

"Hi Charlie, I'm Finn, nice to meet you."

"Are you ' *The*' Finn that designed the improvements to the US F. O'Shea?"

"That's me," I said with a shy grin.

"It's pretty impressive, young man!"

All the crew were helping to move all the packages. As I arrived at the lab, I overheard Don say, "Now that the supplies are here, stage 1 of the take-over is complete." They followed this with a fist bump. They did not realise that I had heard them. I carried on bringing in the box I was carrying and pretended I had only just arrived.

Chapter 8: All is not what it seems!

Back at the hotel, the children were up early trying to follow the clues. Alyssa had joined them after breakfast. She knew all the major highways and a lot about the local area.

"I thought your family had just moved here," said Kieran.

"Well, it is just me and my dad," she corrected.

"I know a lot about Orlando because my cousins live here, so I've been here for most of my holidays."

"Jean-Luca has been looking for any writing in the photos and has a list of places that are in the photos," said Kristina.

"Kieran and I have been using this mapping programme to try to find out if any of these places are on interstate highway routes out of town."

"Each time we have a lead, we look it up online to see if we can find the buildings in the picture," she continued.

"The trouble is that not all of the places are on the same route... It's like the thief is zig-zagging across all the routes!" said Kieran.

"I don't think that is possible," said Alyssa.

"Look at the maps, the connecting roads are so small, they are likely to be dirt roads, that would be very hard to drive on with a giraffe!"

"Do you have any other ideas?" asked Kieran.

"Mmmmm," she said tugging at her hair.

"Do you recognise any of the places in these photos?" asked Jean-Luca.

"Yes," she said. "That one and that one. They are both in Orlando."

"Well, that does not make any sense," said Kristina.

"Why not?" asked Alyssa.

"Because these are the last 2 pictures the thief posted."

"That would mean…" said Jean-Luca.

"Yes," said Kristina, "that would mean he has gone nowhere!"

Kristina flopped back in her chair.

"So, either he went on a circular trip, or he posted the photos in the wrong order on purpose."

"What can we see from the reflection in the giraffe's eyes?"

"On it," said Kieran who was already blowing up the images.

"It is too blurry in the first one…

….but the other four are very clear," said Kieran.

"Here, take a look!"

They all crowded around the screen looking at the images.

"That is clearly a fast-food restaurant," said Jean-Luca.

"Yes. I recognise the big letter 'B'," said Alyssa.

"Although that's not particularly helpful as those burger joints are everywhere," she continued.

"This reflection looks like branding from a shopping mall."

"The next one is just a reflection of a car," said Kieran, so that is not helpful.

"What type of car?" said Kristina.

"Can you see the registration?" asked Jean-Luca.

"Is it parked or driving?"

"Whoaa not so fast," said Kieran.

"We need every little detail!" said Kristina.

"It looks like it is parked, but I can't be sure," said Kieran.

"The other one is the reflection of a large number 21!" said Kieran. "It looks like a marking on a post box of a house."

"That's pretty specific!"

"It could be in any city?" said Jean-Luca.

"But it should be opposite whatever is in the picture with the giraffe," said Kieran, starting to zoom in on the background of the picture.

Kristina was looking at the street view around all the Burger joints. The area opposite the sign looked nothing like what was around the baby giraffe.

"This makes no sense," said Kristina.

"None of it makes sense!" said Alyssa.

She had plotted out where all the photos had been taken.

"Even if we ignore the order, there is not enough time for the thief to drive between these locations."

"I've got it!" shouted Kieran.

"What?" they all crowded around Kieran.

The pictures were zoomed-in so much that they could see each pixel on the photos on Kieran's screen.

"What are we looking at?" asked Jean-Luca.

"You see this change in colour and intensity here at the edge of the giraffe?"

"Yes."

"Well, that means the giraffe has been cut out and pasted onto the backgrounds," said Kieran.

"So that means none of the backgrounds are relevant," said Kristina.

"Exactly," said Kieran. "Total fakes! Pretty good ones too."

"Rabbits on a bicycle!!!" shouted Jean-Luca.

"What?" asked Alyssa.

"I'm not allowed to swear," sighed Jean-Luca.

"You have **got** to come up with something better than that!" said Kieran shaking his head in disbelief.

"That means we have been wasting our time," said Alyssa.

"No," exclaimed Kristina. "It means we have the answer!"

Chapter 9: Stuck!

Sleeping was another challenge in space. There was no lying down to sleep, you could sleep in any direction. I was given a sleep station that had a sleeping bag that was tied to the sides of the pod. It was a good thing that I didn't mind small spaces. I took out my phone and found a voice message from my friends. I could use my phone because there was WIFI at the space station, so it still worked. I clicked on the message to open it and a song burst out of his phone at max volume:

"When you're floating round in space...

...and it hits you in the face...

...diarrhoea!

...diarrhoea!"

I tried to quickly switch it off, but couldn't get it to stop and it went around again:

"When you're floating round in space...

...and it hits you in the face..."

I could hear Kieran laughing and singing with all his might! I had texted them earlier about how hard it was to go to the toilet... and this is what they had sent back! 'Not helpful!' I thought.

Imagining all my friends on Earth rolling around with laughter, I grinned and wrote back, "Ha! Ha! Hilarious!" followed by:

"When you're sitting in the car...

...and the toilet's just too far...

... diarrhoea!

... diarrhoea!"

Then I sent a picture I had taken of the Earth from space.

Even though it was a little weird in the space bed, I fell into a deep sleep really quickly. It had been a really intense 24 hours! I woke in the night to hear raised voices but I couldn't quite make out what they were saying.

This along with the strange interaction I had overheard between the crew earlier made me feel really uneasy. When I woke in the morning though, I was not sure if it had all been a dream.

I decided not to say anything to Captain Lerato, but that I would keep my eyes and ears open. I was given a tour of the research lab where the crew had set up a mini-lab to grow food.

"This is our food wall," said Charlie.

The lettuce was growing out of a sponge-like thing that held onto the water droplets and provided nutrients.

There was only a small hole where the plant stems exited the plastic containers with the sponge.

The containers were hanging vertically to save space, but the plants grew out sideways towards a lightbulb that was placed next to the vegetable wall. This looked a bit strange, but as there was no gravity, there was no reason to grow things vertically.

"We wanted to set up hydroponics, but it is a little technical with all the water," said Charlie.

"Mm Hmm," I said, nodding my head in agreement.

I fully understood the liquid issues in space after my toilet experience...

"Anything to have fresh salad on our plate," said Charlie.

I wasn't terribly fond of lettuce and wasn't sure why anyone would be.

"My friend Kristina would love this!" I said. "She's a vegetarian."

"Would you like me to take a picture of you next to the wall so you can show it to Kristina when you're back home?" asked Charlie.

"Sure. That would be great!" I said.

After 2 days at the station, the crew were preparing to return to Earth. This time, Jo would be the captain on the way home. Captain Lerato was going to be staying on at the space station for the next 4 months.

I had been thinking about what Don had said about taking over the space station, but I was not sure what it meant and now I also wasn't even sure what I had heard. Everyone seemed to get along really well and to be working as a team.

I was already suited and ready to board the rocket home when Captain Lerato came over to say goodbye.

"All ready to go?" she said, with a kind smile.

I tried to talk, but my mouth was dry and only a few 'ums' came out. I wanted to tell Captain Lerato about what I had heard.

"It's OK to feel a little nervous," she said.

"I'm not nervous," I said confused.

"Great!" she said with a smile. "Then in you get."

I settled into my seat and pulled on the straps. Jo tested that it was tight enough and adjusted my straps like I was a baby being strapped into a car seat!

I thought this was a little pointless. If we were going down in this rocket, no amount of tightening the seatbelt was going to save me.

The doors shut and we were now in our sealed pod again.

"All checks complete," said Jo next to me.

Captain Lerato was now on the other end of the mic.

"You are good to go," said Captain Lerato. "Safe journey and nice to have you with us, Finn."

"You are clear for take-off, over."

Captain Jo started the engine.

"Commencing detachment," she said, beginning the release protocol to detach the rocket from the space station.

There was a loud grinding sound.

"That does not sound good!" said Captain Lerato.

"Detachment protocol incomplete," said Jo.

"Can you repeat that, Jo?" said Captain Lerato.

"The rocket won't detach!"

"Start the sequence again," said Captain Lerato.

"Initiating release protocol," said Jo.

My heart started racing... something was not right! Had the rocket docking station been damaged when we landed, or did this have something to do with what I had heard Don saying?

Chapter 10: Back on Earth

Later, back on Earth, there was a video on the news of Finn floating off into space being shown on repeat.

"Guys, come check this out!" shouted Kristina.

Jean-Luca's dad walked in and they bombarded him with questions.

"What is going on?"

"Why is Finn floating about outside the station?"

"Has he got a safety line?"

"Is the rocket damaged?"

"**Slow down!** Slow down! What are you talking about?" asked Jean-Luca's dad.

"Look there! Finn is drifting off into space!" exclaimed Jean-Luca.

His dad frowned at the TV.

"Look!" he said again.

"I can see," said Jean-Luca's dad sounding unsure.

"Finn is tethered to the space station by that umbilical cord thingy."

"Umbilical cord thingy!?!?" asked Jean-Luca.

"Look, there is the cord, so there is no need to panic."

Jean-Luca's dad did look worried though and immediately went to the other room to phone Jean-Luca's mom.

The news feed went to static and the newsreader said, "We seem to have lost the connection to the space station."

"But I'm sure everything is fine up there."

Kristina, Kieran and Jean-Luca sat with their mouths open staring at the television screen that had now changed to a different story.

A few moments later, Jean-Luca's dad came out. "What are you all gawking at?" he asked, looking at the screen that now had soccer on it.

"Never mind," he said "It's time for dinner."

"We can't eat!" exclaimed Kieran, Kristina and Jean-Luca together.

"Finn is fine," he said.

"One of the hatches got stuck and Finn was the smallest one up there and so he was asked to go out to try to fix it."

"See, so there is nothing to worry about," he added.

"But... he has no training!" said Kieran.

"And we don't know if he got back in OK!" said Jean-Luca.

"I'm sure they explained to him what he needed to do and that he is back inside safe and sound by now."

"That is so amazing!" shouted Kristina. "Imagine that! Floating out in space."

She flung herself back onto the bed in a star shape.

"What?" exclaimed Jean-Luca. "Don't you realise how serious this is?"

"The astronauts know what they are doing, they aren't going to let anything happen to Finn," said Kristina. "He's probably having the best time ever!"

"Come on, it is time to get something to eat. We're going somewhere different tonight," said Jean-Luca's dad.

"Where?" they chorused.

"I have booked an Italian restaurant," said Jean Luca's dad.

"Meatballs here I come!" said Kieran.

"Can we check the news on your phone while we are at dinner?" asked Kristina.

"Sure," said Jean-Luca's dad. "Let's go!"

Again, Jean-Luca's mom joined us for dinner, but Finn's parents did not. They were now staying at the base station, being updated on the situation with Finn in real-time. Jean-

Luca's mom was supporting them during the daytime.

When she arrived at the restaurant, she looked tired and concerned. She spoke in hushed tones to Jean-Luca's father at one end of the table while the children tried to listen to what they were saying.

"I can't hear anything," said Kieran.

"It's no use, the restaurant noise is too loud!" said Jean-Luca.

They looked at the menus instead.

"I'm having the meatballs," said Kieran.

"We know... you already told us," said Jean-Luca.

"No need to be snappy!" said Kieran.

"Sorry, I'm worried about Finn," said Jean-Luca.

"What are you having?" Kieran asked, turning to Kristina.

"I'm having the vegetarian lasagne," she said. "It is my absolute favourite!"

"What about you Jean-Luca?" asked Kristina.

"I think I'll also try the lasagne if you think it will be good."

They ordered their meals from a waiter that looked quite distracted. He kept looking around like he was expecting something to happen.

"This vegetable lasagne is amazing!" said Jean-Luca.

"I know," said Kristina, "It's always good!"

"But I don't normally eat vegetables!" said Jean-Luca in amazement.

They were all really hungry, so for a few moments, the table was quiet.

While they were eating, Kristina cleared her throat and said, "I know that we are all worried about Finn right now, but we need to figure out where the baby giraffe is."

"What do you suggest we do next?" asked Kieran shovelling a meatball into his mouth.

"I think it is time we head over to the scene of the crime and retrace the thief's footsteps," said Kristina,

"They are not going to let us head off to the other side of Orlando while Finn is floating off into space!" said Kieran.

"Well, we can't really do anything to help Finn from down here can we?!?!" said Jean-Luca.

"You need to ask your folks if we can go to the cinema tomorrow over here," said Kristina, pointing to a map on his phone.

"OK. I will ask them later," said Jean-Luca.

Before he had a chance to ask, Jean-Luca's mom said, "Tomorrow, all the adults will be going back to the communication centre, so we are arranging a babysitter for you."

"A babysitter?" said Jean-Luca furiously.

"Why can't we come?" asked Kristina.

"Things are complicated," said Jean-Luca's mom. "We need to be there..."

"... and no, you can't all come to the control centre!"

"Can we go to the movies instead?" blurted Jean-Luca.

His mom looked at him surprised.

"How can you be even thinking about going to the movies at a time like this?" she asked.

"We're **Soooooo** bored sitting around in the hotel all day!" whined Jean-Luca.

Jean-Luca's dad put his hand on his mom's arm.

"It might be a good idea," he said. "They have all been cooped up in the hotel for a long time! Why don't we see if the babysitter can take them?"

They all seemed to be holding their breath.

"OK... if she is happy to take 3 children to the movies, they can go."

They all started smiling and chatting again.

"But you will need to listen very carefully to her and stay together!" she added.

Chapter 11: Drifting

As I drifted away from the space station, I froze, unable to move a muscle. It felt like I was in a weird sort of dream. I wondered how I had ended up in this situation which may be the end of the end.

"To infinity and beyond!" I whispered to myself, looking around at the dark expanse of space stretched out in all directions.

"Finn"

"Finn!"

"Finn!"

"Can you hear me?"

"Uh"

"... yes!"

"I can hear you," I said still in a dream-like state.

"Can you pull yourself along the cord back towards the station?" said Captain Lerato.

"Sure," I said.

Carefully I pulled myself slowly along the cord being very gentle so I didn't disconnect myself from the station.

It felt really strange being weightless, surrounded by nothing but... space! It was so dark and quiet with the most beautiful diamond-like twinkling stars everywhere. So many more than I had ever seen from Earth. It was so different being outside the spaceship where there was no glass window to look through. In every direction, there was just vast empty space.

'My mom is really not going to be happy about this,' I thought.

My mom was always trying to make sure that I did not do anything dangerous. As the thought crossed my mind, I realised how ridiculous it was since this really was now a life-or-death situation. If my line snapped, I could float off into space never to be found again, and if we didn't get the docking station fixed, I may never get back to Earth either! So, on balance, I shouldn't be in too much trouble with Mom. Captain Lerato interrupted my thought reel.

"Can you point your visor towards the damaged area so that I can get a better look?" asked Captain Lerato.

"Can you see now?"

"Perfect," said Captain Lerato.

"It looks like we need to fix the bent docking arm," said Captain Lerato.

Finn had been given a tool belt with a rivet gun, a hammer, a screwdriver and a small welder. This was pretty dangerous but necessary to fix any rips in the metal. It was kind of like a soldering iron but only bigger and more dangerous. There was no gas canister, only electricity to heat it. He would never have been given this as a child on Earth, but he was the only one small enough to fit into the space that was damaged and so was going to have to do his best.

"Finn, I need you to be really careful," said Captain Lerato.

This went without saying, as it was awkward to try to do anything while floating around in zero gravity in a marshmallow suit.

"Before you start anything Finn, I need you to clip yourself to the station using the carabiner clip," said Captain Lerato.

"Done."

"OK, fire up the welder," said Captain Lerato.

I switched it on and started repairing the damage to the outer metal around the docking station. It was really slow going, and I had to concentrate very hard. After I had repaired about a third of the damage, I switched it off to take a break.

"How does that look?" I asked Captain Lerato.

"That looks good. Keep going the whole way along the crack," she said.

I was sweating in my helmet, but couldn't wipe the sweat that was now dripping down the side of my face.

I switched the welder back on to start again.

As I switched it on, an explosion rocked the space station.

"Aaagh!" I shouted out as the station rocketed towards me, hitting me hard, and knocking the welder out of my hands.

There was no sound from the explosion because of the empty vacuum of space, but I saw a flash of bright light that flooded my visor hurting my eyes.

I could now only hear static on my comms.

"Come in, come in…"

"Can you hear me Captain Lerato?"

I tapped on my helmet.

"Can you hear me?"

"Can you hear me?"

"Anyone there?"

There was nothing, only the sound of my own voice.

I was on my own!

Chapter 12: All in the eyes!

Alyssa wasn't allowed to join us to go to the movies as her dad was taking her to see their new house. This was a bit of a problem as she knew loads about all of the local shops and was really good at understanding the maps. When we arrived at the movies, we were all looking around trying to see if we could recognise the other landmarks nearby. The babysitter's name was Stacy. She had only just finished school and had said to Jean-Luca's dad when she arrived that she was saving to go travelling around Europe. Jean-Luca's mom had looked a little unsure because Stacy was quite young, but there were not that many options available.

"Be good," she said to the children as they headed out the door.

"So, we have tickets for the morning movie?" said Stacy looking down at the tickets Jean-Luca's mom had given her.

"Yes," said Jean-Luca, "for the first movie at 11 am this morning."

"Well, we'll need to get going soon, as there is quite a lot of traffic."

"OK," we chimed together.

"We're ready," said Kristina shouldering her backpack.

"Why did you choose this movie house, it is so far away from your hotel!" asked Stacy.

"We wanted to see the city," said Kristina quickly.

"But this is so far away, it is outside the city!"

"We thought we could see the city on the drive," said Kieran, thinking quick.

"Mmmm," she said.

When they arrived at the movies, the parking lot was mostly empty.

Stacy was not sure why the kids were so distracted wandering off in different directions and looking around continuously.

"Come on kids, we're going to be late!" she said.

"That's OK," said Kieran, "We don't like watching the ads anyway."

Kristina wandered off towards the edge of the car park without Stacy noticing.

"Oh, come on!" she said, finally noticing that Kristina was missing.

"Where's Kristina gone now?" she asked throwing up her hands.

"No idea," said Jean-Luca pretending not to be interested.

"Come on kids you need to help me find Kristina?"

"Aaaagh!" she grunted, looking around frantically.

Just then, Kristina returned with a grin on her face looking triumphant.

"Where did you run off to?" asked Stacy her voice raised and obviously irritated.

"I just needed to go to the toilet," said Kristina.

"OK. OK. Just let me know if any of you need to go anywhere again," she said. "We need to stick together!" she said, looking visibly shaken.

"Come on, hurry up, we are late now," said Stacy.

They went into the movie, filing in, and taking their seats.

Kristina told them about what she had seen and they started trying to make sense of everything while the movie was playing.

"Ssshhh!"

"You kids really are unbelievable!"

"Just watch the movie!" she said.

As we were leaving the movie, Kristina asked, "Can we go and get some lunch at that burger joint over there with the big 'B'?"

"It doesn't look very healthy," said Stacy unsure.

"Pleeease!!!" they begged.

"We NEVER get burgers in Ireland," said Kieran.

This was clearly untrue, but Stacy did not know this, and it finally persuaded her.

"OK," she agreed.

"Why not?"

The kids were still looking around continuously.

"You kids are really fidgety!" she said. "Can you sit still!"

They were all so excited with all the pieces starting to fall into place. They had started looking out for the thief and his van and half expecting a giraffe to walk across the car park.

"OK," said Kristina. "We'll come clean!"

Stacy looked a little bored until they started explaining the story.

"Today's trip was not about the movies...." Kristina started.

"We've looked at all the photo's posted by the *giraffe snatcher*, and they all point to right here!" said Kieran, pointing to the table.

"This table?" asked Stacy.

"No… not this exact table!" said Kristina. "Somewhere near here!"

"Well, it all makes sense now," she said.

"OK, show me what you've got."

They showed her the zoomed-in reflections in the giraffe's eyes. As they were sitting at an outside table eating lunch, it was hard to see the screens because of the glare. Kieran held the image of the place where they were sitting up first twisting it to match the lettering on the front of the restaurant.

"So, we are at the first location, here," said Kristina pointing to the picture of the giraffe's zoomed-in eyes.

"The second location is that shopping mall there and then we have a third location that I can't see from here."

Kieran slid the third picture over to Stacy.

"We don't know where the third picture is taken from," said Kristina.

"Can we drive around to see if we can find the third location?" asked Jean-Luca.

"Sure, we don't have anything else to do... let's go looking for a criminal!" said Stacy rolling her eyes.

"Can you drive in a spiral from where we are?" asked Jean-Luca.

"Well no.." said Stacy, "the roads don't work that way."

"I'll tell you which roads to take, so we can go through them systematically," said Kieran.

"What are we looking for?"

"A big van or a warehouse large enough to hide a giraffe!"

They drove around aimlessly for 10 minutes.

"Over there!" shouted Kieran, pointing to a large warehouse.

They parked on the road and walked slowly towards the entrance.

"There!" said Kristina.

"What? I can't see anything!" said Jean-Luca.

"Look, spoor!" said Kristina.

"What's spoor?" asked Stacy.

All of them just looked at her.

"Giraffe footprints!" said Kristina after a beat.

"Oh!" she said. "It's time to call the police."

While we waited for the police to come, the giraffe snatcher arrived in his van and pulled into the warehouse. He strolled into the warehouse not noticing the children who were now hiding in the bushes.

After about 10 minutes, the police went up to the warehouse and started to peer in the windows, not sure they were at the right location. The snatcher snuck out of the side door and started to run. He was running straight towards the children. Kristina stuck her foot out of the bush she was hiding in as he ran past.

CRASH!!! the snatcher went flying!

The police sprinted towards them and handcuffed him before he could get up! The children jumped out of the bushes high-fiving each other and whooping!

Reporters and a news crew seemed to appear out of nowhere. Now, Kristina, Kieran and Jean-Luca were also on the news. "How did you kids catch the giraffe snatcher?" asked an enthusiastic reporter.

"We worked together and followed the clues," said Kieran.

"We really couldn't have done it without our friend Alyssa," Kristina said, hoping Alyssa was watching the news.

"...but many adults weren't able to catch the snatcher!"

"Well, we had nothing else to do in our hotel while we waited for our friend to get back from space!"

"What?" asked the reporter. "Are you friends with Finn O'Shea?".

"Yes. We came over here together from Ireland to watch the launch!"

"Well, we all hope for his speedy and safe return..." said the reporter.

"...and now onto our next story which has footage of Finn fixing the rocket docking station."

"Wait..." said the reporter holding his earpiece into his ear, trying to hear what he was being told.

"We have breaking news," he said.

"There seems to have been an explosion at the space station!"

"This story is just getting wilder every day, Tom!"

"What?" demanded Kristina.

The TV crew quickly moved the children away from the reporter who was live on air. The children ran over to one of the media trucks that had a screen, so they could watch the news live.

The police bundled the snatcher into the back of their police car. As they pulled off, the car stopped briefly next to them, so that the police could thank the children. It was a hot day and the window to the back was open a crack.

"Why did you do it?" asked Kristina, incredulous as to why anyone would steal a baby giraffe.

"To create a distraction!" he said cryptically.

As the police were driving the snatcher away, he shouted:

"How did you find me?"

Kieran smirked, "It's all in the eyes!"

"It's all in the eyes!"

Chapter 13: What could go wrong?

"Captain Lerato, can you hear me?"

"Captain Lerato..."

There was silence. Not even the crackle of static anymore!

'**Oh great!** I am floating in space trying to fix the space station with No one to help me!' I thought.

I realised that if systems were all failing, I may not be able to get back into the space station. I also only had a small oxygen tank that would run out after a few hours.

I could feel my breathing speeding up and my heart starting to race. I recognised this panicked feeling, and when this happened before at the karate competition, I could not think at all!

"OK breathe," I said out loud to myself.

I started to take deep long breaths blowing them out slowly until my heart had stopped trying to thump itself out of my chest.

"OK, think!"

"Think! Think! Think!"

'It's just like fixing the toaster,' I thought.

I loved taking appliances apart at home and putting them back together, except that I could never get the toaster to work again!

'OK, not the toaster. Bad example,' I thought shaking my head.

'It's just like fixing one of my toy rockets.'

'Except I only get one shot at this!'

"OK, focus!" I said to myself again out loud.

I slowly and calmly started repairing the damage but realised that I did not have everything I needed. Some of the electrical wires had been broken and I needed to fix the connection so that the electronics would work. There were two major problems with this. The first was that I could not hold the wires, or twist them, with the big gloves I was wearing. The second problem was I knew that you can't *play* with live wires without getting electrocuted! Just then Captain Lerato appeared on what looked like a long cord from the other side of the space station.

"Finn, can you hear me?"

"Yes," I replied.

"Boy, am I glad to see you! Why are the comm's not working?"

"They should start working soon," said Captain Lerato, "We had to reboot the system."

"I realised after you showed me the damage, that you were going to need pincer pliers and a second pair of hands. Fixing the electronics will be tricky."

"Exactly," I said with a grin. "I've fixed everything except these wire connections here," I said, pointing to the broken wires.

"OK, let's do it and get back into the station," said Captain Lerato.

"Won't we get electrocuted if we work on the wires?" I asked.

"It's OK. I switched off the circuit for the docking area before I came out," she said.

It was really tricky to hold the small wires still to fix them, while floating around. We had both tried to anchor ourselves, but it was a strange feeling, like doing everything in slow motion.

Captain Lerato had brought two pairs of long-nosed pliers and gave one to me. She also had the tool to strip the insulation on the wires so that we could join the metal together, and electrical tape. It was really tricky work and I felt a bit like a bomb disposal expert that I had seen on TV. A big awkward suit trying to do really delicate and crucial work. If this didn't work, I was not going home anytime soon!

We worked together, stripping the wires, getting ready to join them together. It was slow, tedious work.

Then the pliers dropped out of my hand!

"Nooooo!" I shouted into my helmet.

As it floated away, I saw my chances of getting home getting more and more distant.

Captain Lerato caught the pliers and handed them back to me.

"It's OK," she said. "Let's get this finished."

As we worked, I said, "You know, I have been dreaming about being an astronaut floating around in space for a long time,"

"You and lots of other children around the world," said Captain Lerato with a grin.

"Now I am feeling guilty about wanting to get back home!" I confessed. I missed home and was looking forward to getting my feet back onto solid ground.

"Astronauts train for years to deal with the adjustment, and you had no time to prepare," said Captain Lerato. "Don't worry, you will be wanting to come back to space as soon as you are home," she said with a smile.

"Funny how the grass is always greener on the other side," I said.

"This time, it literally is!" she said, and we both started laughing. "Just look at that amazing Earth!"

"Africa looks so big, it's awesome!" I said.

"My grandfather was from Botswana," said Captain Lerato. "Look, you can see it over there," she said, pointing. "It is the country near the bottom of Africa."

"Why is most of it so brown?" I asked.

"That is because of the Kalahari Desert," said Captain Lerato.

"I'd love to go to Africa someday," I said.

"I've been a few times and it is really such a beautiful country!" she said.

"Now, let's get this circuit fixed, so we can get you home!"

As we worked, we chatted about Captain Lerato's time in space and how things had changed over the years.

"See that satellite over there?" she said, "and there, and there."

"Yes..." I said.

"When I first came up here, there were hardly any satellites... but now they are everywhere!"

Just then Captain Lerato's tether came loose floating slowly away from the spaceship.

"How on Earth did that happen?"

"Well, not on Earth... you know what I mean!"

She reeled it in while holding on to me.

Then, we noticed that mine was also no longer connected to the station.

"What is going on?" she said.

I started to feel the panic again as I began to drift slowly away from the station.

Captain Lerato hit the button on the side of her boots that switched on the electromagnets. She grabbed my lifeline and lifted her feet towards the station. We were pulled towards the station and her boots stuck onto the side.

"That's so cool!" I said.

"They are new, a bit like the magnets that pick up cars in a lot where they crush cars."

I pressed the button on my boots now and also attached myself to the station.

"These will only work while we have battery power," said Captain Lerato.

"...and we don't have too much oxygen left," I said. "I'm below 50% already!"

Captain Lerato looked perplexed.

I wanted to tell her about what I had overheard but wasn't sure where to start, so I just started babbling.

"I think that some of the crew are trying to take over the space station!" I blurted out.

"What!?!" she said.

I had her full attention now.

"We have been working with that team for months, it's not possible!"

I added; "When I arrived and we were unloading the supplies, I overheard Don saying; 'Now that the supplies are here, stage 1 of the take-over is complete.' He didn't know I heard them. Now that we are floating out here, I think it means they're trying to do it!"

Captain Lerato's mind was racing, she was shaking her head and her eyes were darting around.

"There probably isn't any point in trying the comms anymore. I don't think we are going to get any help from inside," she said.

"Can the spaceship be controlled remotely from the base station?" I asked.

"Yes, but we can't communicate with them either," said Captain Lerato.

"I have my phone in my pocket," I said.

Captain Lerato looked confused.

"I'm a kid... I never go anywhere without my phone," I said.

"OK, but I'm not sure how that helps," said Captain Lerato.

"Well, I have been texting my friends in Orlando using the space station WIFI to make calls," I said.

"But how do we get it out of your pocket or dial the numbers, if you take your phone out of your suit, it will freeze and so will you!"

I started to wriggle and squirm in my suit. My suit was a little bit too big, making it fairly easy for me to get my arms out of the sleeves and into the body of my suit. The suit arms looked ridiculously floppy now. I retrieved my phone from my pocket and switched it on. We heard the very exciting sound of the phone starting up. The problem was pushing buttons without being able to see the screen.

I said, "Siri, phone Kristina!"

Nothing happened, no response.

"Siri can't hear you," said Captain Lerato, "you need to get your phone into your helmet."

I wiggled and jiggled some more and the phone popped up into my helmet.

"Siri, phone Kristina!"

"I'm sorry, the mobile you are trying to call is switched off!"

"Oh, **come on!**" I exclaimed.

"Try one of your other friends," said Captain Lerato.

"Siri, phone Kieran!"

The phone started ringing. I had never been so happy to hear that ring tone.

Kieran answered, "Hey Finn, we got the giraffe snatcher and we were on TV!"

"Awesome!" I said.

"It was SO great!" said Kieran starting to tell the story of their day.

"We're in a bit of trouble up here and we need your help," I said, cutting him off.

"What kind of trouble?" said Kieran, his tone of voice changing.

"Are you with Kristina and Jean-Luca?" I asked.

"Yes," he said.

"Can you put me on speakerphone?"

I explained our situation, in short, quick sentences, as I was worried that my battery might run out.

"But what can we do from down here?" asked Kieran.

"I need you to go over to the base station and hack into the space station computer!" I said.

"Sure, no problem," said Jean-Luca, "that should be easy!"

I could hear the sarcasm in Jean-Luca's voice.

"I know you can do it," I said. I have a plan. "When you get there, just tell the adults that you are bored and ask for a computer that you can use to play computer games. I will give you

Captain Lerato's password and we can figure out how to get us back into the space station."

"Why can't you just phone an adult to do this?"

"Because they will never believe me and I can't exactly pass the phone to Captain Lerato!"

"Also, they will try to contact the crew on the space station and that would let them know our plan. They will also deny that there is any problem up here if they have already taken over the station."

"We don't have a lot of time because our oxygen is running out, so you need to hurry!"

I gave them Captain Lerato's password in case I couldn't get through later and then hung up.

Chapter 14: Need for Speed

Finn's life was in their hands now! They now needed to persuade Stacy to take them to the base station. Kristina simply walked over to her and said, "Can you take us over to the space centre?"

"Your parents told me to bring you back to the hotel," she said.

"Yes, but something has come up and we need to go to my parents," said Jean-Luca.

"I'm not sure," she said, "I don't think they are going to let you in."

"Look. It is literally a matter of life or death!" said Kristina.

"... and we need to hurry!"

She wasn't looking convinced.

"OK," said Kieran, "let's get into the car and we can explain on the way."

Telling her the full story the last time had worked, so as they drove, they explained everything including the phone call, leaving out the bit where they were planning to hack into the space centre's computer network.

Stacy was driving normally at what seemed like the slowest pace through the traffic. They were all fidgeting and feeling stressed, knowing that Finn's oxygen was running out, while they dawdled through the traffic.

"Can't you go any faster?" asked Kieran in frustration.

"I'm not going to get a speeding fine for another one of your wild goose chases," she said. It seems they didn't quite have Stacy on board with their plan.

"Jean-Luca, can you phone your mom to ask her to arrange for the guard to let us through the gate?" asked Kristina.

"She is not answering," said Jean-Luca.

"Anyone have Finn's parent's number?"

"I only have Finn's number," said Kieran.

The traffic was heavy and Kieran, who was sitting in front, was drumming his fingers on the dashboard.

"Aaaagh!" exclaimed Kristina as we hit another red light.

Jean-Luca tried his mom's number again.

'*The mobile phone you have dialled has been switched off,*' came the automated voice.

He tried his dad:

'*The mobile phone you have dialled has been switched off.*'

"I think we are on our own!" he said to the others.

They finally arrived at the gate to the space centre.

"Hi kids!" said the guard recognising them.

"Are you here for another tour?"

"No, we need to go up to the control centre to my parents," said Jean-Luca

"Mmm," said the guard thoughtfully.

"The last time I let you in, your friend stowed away in a rocket!"

"Could you call Jade and let us speak to her?" asked Kristina.

He seemed to think this was a good idea and called her on his radio. The guard had been very friendly, smiling at them and enjoying the banter.

When he spoke to Jade, his face seemed to freeze and his expression changed. He now looked very worried. He leaned over into the car window.

"Jade will meet you at the entrance to the control centre," he said.

He explained where we should go and tapped the car twice and we were through. The change in his voice and facial expression worried Kristina. She looked back as they drove through. The guard was shaking his head slowly, as he watched them drive up to the building.

Jade was waiting for them. She also had a sad look on her face. Jade ushered them into the foyer putting her arm around Kristina protectively, as they walked. Jean-Luca's mom and dad were waiting for them just inside.

"Thank you for bringing them to us, Stacy. We really appreciate you looking after the children today." Jean-Luca's dad paid her and she walked back to her car.

Jean-Luca's parents sat them all down and Jade went off to get some drinks for everyone.

"I'm afraid we have some bad news!" said Jean-Luca's dad.

Before anyone could respond, Jean-Luca's mom said, "We have lost Finn!"

"No, No, No!" said Kieran, and all the children started talking at once.

"It is NOT true!"

"It is true, the second in command of the space shuttle told us that they have drifted off into space! We spoke directly to one of the crew members."

"Is his name Don?"

"Yes."

"He is lying!!!!"

Jean-Luca's mom put up her hand, "We know this is very upsetting!"

"But it is **NOT** true!" insisted Kristina.

Jean-Luca's parents thought the children were just in denial and didn't believe that something bad had happened to their friend.

"Stay with Jade," they said, "we need to go and find Finn's parents."

When Jade returned with their drinks, Kristina turned on the tears.

"We don't want to be here with everyone..." she sobbed. "Please can we go somewhere quiet?"

Jade looked at Kristina, a gentle look on her face. She looked around the room. Lots of staff were having coffee in the canteen and it was very noisy.

"OK," she said. "Let's go to my office."

Her office was big with a desk and a small circular meeting table with five chairs around it. She settled them at the table and said, "I have a few things I need to do. Jean-Luca, I'll tell your parents you are here, and I will be back in half an hour."

Jade smiled weakly and left the room.

They waited until they couldn't hear her footsteps anymore before daring to move. Kristina sprang into action and settled behind the computer at Jade's desk.

"Login?" she demanded.

"Password?"

Kieran spelt it out from the note he had written on his phone. Kristina's fingers were flying across the keys.

Kristina could touch-type and it seemed she was typing so fast, that her fingers were a blur on the keyboard.

"Give Finn a missed call," she ordered, "...one ring only, he needs to call us back."

Jean-Luca was looking over her shoulder.

Kristina was listing all the drives and directories using command line codes, familiarising herself with the network structure.

"There, that looks like the right drive," said Jean-Luca. "Try that one."

As she navigated the system using command line through the terminal, she tried to access the drive.

There was a beep that sounded more like a honk...

"Access denied!"

"Try logging in as a 'superuser' with the root password," said Jean-Luca.

"But we don't have that password," said Kristina.

"Try Captain Lerato's login and password... people often use the same one," said Kieran.

"Unlikely, but I will try it," said Kristina.

And just like that, they were in!

"I think we might be committing a federal crime," said Kieran, with what seemed like a little bit of excitement in his voice.

"We are only kids and we have permission from Captain Lerato," said Jean-Luca.

"I don't care!" said Kristina, "we are saving Finn and that is final! Now focus!"

"Open that file," said Jean Luca.

Kristina entered the command to open the file - 'space_station_blueprint.xcf' and a detailed plan pinged up on the screen with all the details, dimensions and codes.

"Excellent!"

"Now all we need to do is to figure out how to access the station remotely to unlock the door," said Jean-Luca.

The phone rang.

"Finn, are you OK?"

"Yes, but we are running low on oxygen!"

"We're into the system," blurted Kieran.

"You guys are **amazing!**" I said.

"We need you to open the hatch closest to us."

"Which one is that?" asked Kristina.

"The door has J-10 C42 written on it," I said.

"I've got it on the blueprint," said Kristina. "But how do we open it from all the way over here?"

I asked Captain Lerato if she knew.

"Captain Lerato said you need to access the _remote override protocol_."

Kristina typed in:

'Sudo spacestation remote override' and pressed enter.

The computer replied.

"Are you sure you want to remotely access the space station?"

Kristina typed 'yes'.

"We're in!" shouted Jean Luca a little too loud.

"We're not though, and we're running out of oxygen," I said. "You need to be quick!".

The door to the office opened.

"What are you kids doing?"

demanded Jade, rushing over to them.

"Saving Finn!"

"What? You can't be accessing my computer!" said Jade. "How did you log in? Out of the way."

"NO!" said Jean Luca, blocking her way.

"We are on the phone to Finn," added Kieran.

"What?" asked Jade.

"Finn, can you talk to Jade?"

"No! You need to open the hatch right now... Captain Lerato has run out of oxygen!"

"She's passed out... you need to do it now!" he screamed.

"We don't know how to!"

"Try using the command 'open'," said Kieran.

Kristina typed:

'Open J-10 C42'

Jade had frozen, not sure what to do.

"It's working," I said.

"Get her into the hatch," said Jade, stating the obvious.

I pressed the button to disconnect my magnetic boots from the station. I took the tether that was supposed to connect me to the station and tied it around Captain Lerato's waist, hit the button on her boots and then pulled us both into the hatch.

"Close it!" I shouted as we got inside.

As the hatch closed, I ripped off my helmet.

In Jade's office, all they could hear was Finn's mobile clattering to the floor as it fell out of his helmet.

"Finn?"

"Finn?"

"Are you OK?"

I ripped the pipe from the back of my oxygen tank, filling the airlock with oxygen. I gasped, and grabbed Captain Lerato and removed her helmet.

"She's not waking up!" I yelled.

"Finn, this is Jade speaking, put Captain Lerato on her side and make sure her airway is clear."

After what seemed like eternity...

...she started to gasp.

Chapter 15: All tied up!

She was groaning a bit and I was by her side rubbing her back and trying to get her to wake up.

"Captain Lerato..."

"Captain Lerato, you need to wake up," I was saying, now in a whisper.

Before she had had time to wake up, the door to the space station opened. Standing in the doorway was Don! It seemed like all of the blood in my body went to my toes!

I backed away from Captain Lerato, moving to the side of the airlock. Don ignored me, perhaps thinking I was not a threat because I am a kid. He moved over to Captain Lerato and covered her mouth. She immediately woke up and started to struggle.

I took my helmet off and smashed it into Don's head as hard as I could!

"Take that! you rotten crook!" I roared with anger pumping through my veins. He flew into the wall and then floated off, knocked out cold.

Captain Lerato, was recovering, still taking deep breaths. "Thanks, Finn. You really are a lifesaver!" she said.

"Can you find plastic zip ties on your utility belt?" she asked, still gasping for breath.

I quickly looked through all the Velcro pockets and found the largest size. I tied Don's hands and feet together before he could wake up. I also made a second loop tying him to the rail in the airlock.

Captain Lerato leaned back against the side of the airlock breathing slowly.

"He is friends with 2 other crew members on this ship," said Captain Lerato. "We need to find them quickly!"

I was quite tired all of a sudden after all the action, but I knew we needed to arrest the other crew before we would be safe.

"Ready Finn?"

"Let's go!"

Captain Lerato hit the button to open the airlock.

We moved slowly towards the control room where we found one of the other crew members.

"Where's Don?" he demanded, shocked to see them.

"We're doing fine, thank you," replied Captain Lerato.

He headed off towards the airlock, but Captain Lerato caught his feet...

"Oh no you don't!" she said.

He started to wriggle and struggle, but I grabbed his arm and bent it backwards by jamming his body against the side panel using his whole body to pin him down.

Captain Lerato quickly reached for the plastic zip ties and tied up his hands and feet.

"Two down, one to go!"

At that moment, the third accomplice arrived... it was getting crowded in the small space. We thrust the man we had just tied up towards her, knocking her off course. Captain Lerato yanked on her feet, pulling her fast towards us. At that moment, I caught her arms. Both Captain Lerato and I had anchored our own feet to the side rails. We quickly bound her with the zip ties, and then relaxed.

"Time for tea?" Captain Lerato said.

For anyone not on board, this would seem absurd... but we really did now need a cup of tea to calm our nerves.

Captain Lerato made the tea and we quietly drank it for a moment while the other crew members buzzed around. Captain Lerato put 2 spoons of sugar in both of our cups which was sickly sweet, but I had started to shake, so this was exactly what I needed.

Jo arrived and Captain Lerato and I explained what had happened. "Where was the rest of the crew?" Captain Lerato asked. "They locked us all into the lab. We have only just managed to escape. We had to remove the door completely to get out," said Jo.

"We need to get these guys back to Earth," she said, gesturing to the astronauts who were tied up. She shook her head. "I just don't know how this could have happened!"

They loaded up the astronaut gang into the rocket. They were all swearing, shouting and resisting as we loaded them. Two were placed in the escape rocket that I had come up in, and one was upfront with us. All the controls on the escape rocket were disabled, so they couldn't cause any more trouble.

I was quite sad to say goodbye to Captain Lerato since we had been through so much together. I was in my astronaut suit, ready to go. She put her arm around my shoulder. "Can we do a call later when I'm back on Earth?" I asked.

"Sure," said Captain Lerato, with a smile. "That would be great."

"Thank you for all your help Finn, you really were a lifesaver!" she said with a wink.

"Later..." I said, holding my hand out for a fist bump.

"Later..." said Captain Lerato, bumping my fist and beaming a smile.

"Ready Finn?" asked Jo.

"I have never been more ready to go!" I said, putting on my helmet.

"Let's go home then...," said Jo.

Later it was discovered that the astronauts who tried to take over the space station were part of an international criminal gang who were trying to gain control over the satellites. This would have given them control of all global communications! Turns out I had saved the world from extortion and decades of control by a criminal gang!

The flight back to Earth was super-fast. I had the best seat at the front with the most amazing view of Earth. I tried to quiet my mind and soak it all up. Earth, the universe, all the stars!!

The entry was a bit rocky with roaring flames flicking past the window. The rocket shook and bumped around so much, I thought it might fall apart!

After entry, as we started to cruise down to Earth, the Captain was talking to the ground crew and turning the rocket, preparing for landing. I looked down over the Earth, taking in the last views.

Landing was always a bit nerve-wracking. The roar of the reverse thruster kicked in and the vibrations were intense until all of a sudden, we were back on Earth.

Jo opened the hatch, and after fumbling to unbuckle my straps, I walked out of the rocket first. As I walked unsteadily down the stairs, the ground staff clapped and cheered and Jean-Luca, Kieran and Kristina ran towards me, jumping on me and giving me a giant hug.

My mom and dad were hot on their heels until everyone was hugging me and I could barely breathe. I saw a tear roll down my dad's cheek and I snuggled in for an extra squeeze.

The authorities had arrived to arrest the three criminal astronauts. They were all still tied up with plastic zip ties.

"We'll need to talk to Finn in the morning," said the chief investigator, "but for now, I think he probably needs some rest."

As we drove back to our hotel, all of us fell asleep like dominoes in the back seat of the car, with our heads all slumped to the one side. It had been a very exhausting day!

When we returned to the base the next morning, Jade had organized a small ceremony. She presented all of us with medals for ingenuity and bravery.

They were bigger than our hands and had a rocket on the front.

The medals were really heavy and shiny,
with each of our names engraved on the back.

"Wow!" said Kieran admiring his medal,

"These are AWESOME!"

"This was the best holiday ever!" exclaimed
Kristina.

... the end.

The Adventures of Finn O'Shea
Book 3: *'Digiboy'*

Chapter 1:

I was moving fast, the wind whipping against my cheeks. It was cold and dark. I was sliding down a long bendy slide, going faster and faster... The slide bent and dipped with no warning. It was pitch, pitch black. So dark I couldn't see my legs. I screamed with every surprising drop, my belly jumping into my throat. I was thrown left and right, then tumbled down to a new level. I was tumbling head over heels out of control bumping against the sides. **"Ouch!"** Immediately the slide turned right and sped up **super**, **super**-fast until I was rolling out of the tunnel into bright light.

"Aaagh!" I moaned as the pain from the light seared into my eyes. The tunnel had been so dark and the light on the platform was so bright that my eyes burned. I was blinking and could barely see anything. It reminded me of summertime when my cousins shone their flashlights in my eyes when we were camping.

The platform was quite small with lots of buttons and switches. I really wanted to press them to see what they all did, but that had got me into trouble before, so I waited.

I was tired and hungry and my clothes were ripped from being tumbled and tossed for hours through the tunnels. The platform was like an island in a sea of tunnel connections that exited out in all directions to what seemed like infinity... and beyond! I knew that I needed to choose a tunnel, but I also needed a rest. I also needed a map... This is what one normally used when one was lost, but it may not even have been useful in this situation, as I was not sure where I was trying to go or where I was.

I sat in the middle considering my options and trying to catch my breath! At first, the buttons all looked the same. There were what seemed like a hundred tunnels going off the giant floating platform. All tunnels headed off into the blackness. After the last trip through the tunnel, I was not that keen to get into another one, but there also did not seem to be anything on the platform except buttons and screens on a control panel in the middle. All of a sudden, the light that shone brightly when I had landed on the platform went out. Immediately I felt sorry that I hadn't quickly examined all the buttons more closely before the lights went off.

I felt through my pockets taking an inventory of what was left. I usually had a small torch, some string, a bit of flint and one or two sweets. My mom wouldn't let me have a penknife, otherwise, I would have had that too. I was *really* hungry and so started to suck on one of the sweets. I felt better straight away and congratulated myself for putting the sweets in my pocket with the zip. If I hadn't, I definitely would have lost them in the tunnels. Although the light from under the platform was still shining, the platform itself was dark and seemed to be floating in a sea of blackness. I fished my torch out of my pocket and tried to switch it on. It did not work! The torch was often didn't work, so I shook it and smacked it with my hand and bright light shot out of the bulb as the batteries connected. Now I moved it slowly and gently across the platform to examine all the controls being careful not to step off the edge.

All the tunnels were covered with what looked like a little door. The doors had no handles, and it was not obvious what you needed to do to open them. Nothing was labelled. The buttons looked the same, the tunnels looked the same so there was no way of knowing which one to pick. I carried on this slow and thorough search of the platform moving from where I had started in a circle around the edge. Then I turned to the middle where there were more buttons on what looked like a control panel.

It was tempting to press the big red button, but I didn't yet dare. I carried on carefully looking at each section slowly. As I examined the control panel, I saw some small letters etched roughly into the plastic next to a square blue button.

It was just one word:

'Digiboy'

"Digiboy!" I said slowly, considering this. Another boy with a penknife had been here I thought. Without thinking anymore, I pressed the button.

About the author

Dr Marian Brennan is both a scientist and a writer living in Wicklow in Ireland. After completing a degree in science, she moved to Dublin to do a PhD. She is passionate about science and storytelling. Her children's novels are fun and exciting and written to spark curiosity and inspire young children.

For updates on new releases:

website: www.marianbrennan.com

Twitter: @marianbrennan

Instagram:@marianbrennan_phd

Printed in Great Britain
by Amazon